T0284154

The LOVE LETTERS of a PORTUGUESE NUN

First published in French in 1669
First published by Hesperus Press in 2023
English language translation by Richard Haydock in 1890
Preface by Albert Piedagnel, 1890
Introduction by Josephine Lazarus, 1899

Designed and typset by Roland Codd

eBook ISBN: 978-1-84391-928-5
Paperback ISBN: 978-1-84391-929-2

All rights reserved. No part of this book may be reproduced in any form or
by any electronic or mechanical means, including information storage and
retrieval systems, without written permission from the author, except for the
use of brief quotations in a book review.

This book is sold subject to the condition that it shall not be resold, lent,
hired out or otherwise circulated without the express prior consent of
the publisher.

Printed in Great Britain by Bell and Bain Ltd, Glasgow

The LOVE LETTERS of a PORTUGUESE NUN

Being the Letters Written by Marianna Alcaforado to
Noël Bouton de Chamilly, Count of St. Leger
(later Marquis de Chamilly), in the year 1668

GABRIEL DE GUILLERAGUES

TRANSLATED BY RICHARD HAYDOCK

INTRODUCTION BY JOSEPHINE LAZARUS

HESPERUS

"Aimer pour être aimé, c'est de l'homme: mais aimer pour aimer, c'est presque de l'ange."
LAMARTINE

CONTENTS

INTRODUCTION

SO FAR AS we know, the Portuguese Letters have never been offered to the public in English dress, and one cannot but rejoice at the opportunity to say a tender word, to lay another wreath as it were upon a grave that will always be green with immortal youth and love.

How far distant their date — 1668! Think of the storms and ravages of time. How many forgotten events! How many things that the world calls solid have perished, and these letters endure! The frail sheets have come down to us through the ages, breathing still the breath of life, of passion, and of pain. How brief too the episode! A few short months, and the dream was ended, the story all told. In order the better to understand it we must call to mind the convent life of the period; the relaxed rule that often prevailed; the social and secular causes which led to its adoption; the worldly relations that were permitted, and in many cases the entire absence of religious character and discipline.

We have no clew as to the circumstances which placed Marianna in the convent, except that she tells us she had been there from childhood. The life was hateful to her, she says, and she had only seen disagreeable people. In her letters we find absolutely no trace of the religious vocation, unless it be in the exalted temperament so fired by her ideal. There is no commingling of devotional ecstacy with the purely earthly attachment to which she abandoned herself; there are no scruples, no remorse or self-accusation; indeed, scarcely the consciousness of sin or wrong-doing. There seems to have been room but for one sentiment in her heart, which was unoccupied, unawake, until her lover came.

She was living her life with languid unconcern and indifference. The French troops were quartered in the neighborhood; a review took place, and she stood with her gay companions watching it from the balcony. A dashing young officer caracoles by, and glances up, observing and observed. He singles out Marianna, or at least so she fancies, and at all events her heart goes out to him never to return.

Apparently he found no great difficulty in penetrating into the convent and gaining access to Marianna, who, from the first, gave herself up with unqualified surrender to the overmastering emotion which awoke new energies and potencies dormant within her. She does not seem to have been disturbed by the scandal of the situation, although she speaks afterwards of the danger he ran in visiting her, of the anger of her parents, and of the strict laws in regard to nuns. But she made no mystery of her passion, on this account; she wished every one to know it; she gloried in it and in the lengths to which it had carried her.

The nuns are in her confidence; the most severe among them, she says, pity and sympathize with her. It is to one of them that she intrusts the package containing the letters and gifts to be returned to her faithless lover, and it is through another French officer that she communicates with him. Lightly as he came, the cavalier has gone again back to his gay life in France, and sporting like a jewel in his cap the treasure he had won, for the letters were evidently given by him for publication during his life-time. No one knew then who had written or received them. Nor has the lover's identity ever yet been clearly established. According to Maurice Paléologue, in the *Revue des Deux Mondes* of October 15, 1889, modern critics have exculpated the Marquis de Chamilly from the charge laid upon him, although St. Simon explicitly names him as the person to whom were addressed "the famous Portuguese Letters, written by a nun he had known in Portugal, who fell madly in love with him."

As to the poor Marianna, her name was discovered accidentally, as late as 1810, on the cover of an old edition, with the inscription: "The nun who wrote these letters was named Marianna Alcaforado, nun at Beja, between Estramadura and Andalusia." Further than this, we know nothing. The letters are the only record we possess. Before and after all is a blank; all her existence is summed up in that single event, and her whole destiny concentrated in the one glowing moment whose rays are carried down to us. Each letter-there are only five of them-has a spark of the divine fire. The last one breaks off abruptly when she finally realizes the absolute hopelessness of her case, and the utter unworthiness of the man to whom she had given her faith. After this, not another word — "the rest is silence," and sorrow that may not be spoken.

And we ask ourselves, what is it in this fragment of a life, this intensely personal experience, that so draws and appeals to us, and that invests with so touching a grace the figure of the forsaken nun? Her fate is not a peculiar one, nor her grief so uncommon, but we have only to turn the pages where her heart is laid bare to discover their sweet and intimate charm, to become aware of the subtle aroma that pervades them, as of the soul's very essence. An indefinable something is there, infinite and eternal, since it may not perish, though human forms that embody it perish, and human hearts break with its over-measure. The girl herself is conscious of an experience that transcends the ordinary. She has touched the central fount of her being; she feels herself able to give endlessly, from a source exhaustless and universal; to give without reserve or limitation, even though giving be in vain. Not to every one is it granted to be capable of such generosity and enthusiasm of devotion, such an "*élan*" of the whole nature. Better even than to be loved, she says, is the power to love with such vehemence. It is surprising to see what changes she can ring upon her single theme, and how with one note, always the same yet always different, her passionate nature vibrates. What desperate longing and loneliness! What transfigured memories! What pathetic appeal and remonstrance! And yet in the midst of her grief, she is grateful to him. Has he not revealed her to herself? Has he not quickened and made alive her sensibilities? She thanks him for her very power of suffering. "You are more to be pitied than I am," she says to the man, who could remain unmoved and indifferent. But she defies him completely to forget her, or ever to content himself with lesser joys and lesser love than she has brought him. How she lingers over the phrases, repeating and insisting — unable to bid him farewell or tear herself from the pages that seem to bring her near to him.

But it is in the last letter that she rises to her full height, and faces the inevitable with dignity and resolution. There is no longer any possibility of self-deception. The illusion is dispelled, the enchantment broken, and she awakes to the bitter reality; the consciousness of his unworthiness, of her own sin, and that the end has come. His letters must be restored to him, with the portrait and bracelets he gave her. She does not trust herself even to write his name on the package; her confidant takes charge of it. It is as though her very heart-strings were being torn from her. Now that the idol has crumbled and proved unworthy of her worship, it is her own passion that she clings to, her love that she loves. What will take the place, she asks herself, of this all-powerful and all-pervading feeling that filled to overflowing every moment of her life, every thought and faculty of her being? More dear to her than any joy, she says, will be the memory of her sorrow. Throughout the letter we feel the interruption of tears-the laying down and taking up of the pen — the inability to write the words that must be spoken. "Oh, if you had only let me go on loving you!" she passionately cries out. But she implores him not to answer her, — not to write and disturb the tranquillity which she hopes to attain; and she suddenly comes to an end, this time without a farewell or a word of tenderness.

Like a broken column the little story stands, a pathetic monument of blighted hopes and unrequited sacrifice. And we, who at this distance feel our sympathies stirred, cannot refrain from the question, is it then a gift, or the greatest of fatalities, this concentration of sensibility, this focusing of vitality upon a single point, which burns and glows before the world? There are tropical temperaments for whom the extreme is the normal, and whose destiny depends upon the control and direction of this excess. To outpour it upon imperfect finite creatures is to place it at the mercy of another, or still worse to throw it back upon self, unused and working misery and ruin. To lead it into broader channels, along the currents of universal and impersonal being, to large unselfish end and purpose is to find for it scope and fulfillment.

The figure of the Portuguese nun glides among the shadows, and other shadows arise — a vision of white-robed and black-robed sisters, the veiled forms of nuns silently winding along, — Heloise is there, for whom heaven itself holds only Abelard — the sainted Theresa with breast pierced by the flame-tipped arrow, symbol of the divine love which has entered her soul — the lovely Louise de la Vallière, the petted favorite of a court, doing penance in solitude and tears for having loved too much, — and how vast a throng besides of ardent and gracious beings, brides of heaven or earth, all alike kindled with the passion, whether mystic or human, which radiates from the inner Life and Light, breathing through the world. Most favored perhaps among women, are ye who have known the keen sorrow and joy of loving, and unto whom it has been promised that many sins should be forgiven. For ye are the Initiate. Earthly love is but the shadow, the presage, perhaps, of the divine. Purified by suffering, made aware through pain and hindrance and passionate unrest that its home is not in human hearts, it breaks the bonds of sense and lifts itself on its own pinions into ideal heights, the realm of spirit and the abode of blessedness and peace.

–Josephine Lazarus, 1899

PREFACE

IN 1663 it became the policy of Louis XIV to help Portugal against Spain; this was done indirectly, however; subsidies were secretly furnished, troops levied, and a crowd of volunteers pressed to the front. Between this little army, commanded by Schomberg, and the poor Spanish army which disputed the field, each summer, much marching and counter-marching took place with very small results. There were many skirmishes and encounters, and among them, perhaps, one victory. Who cares about it to-day? But the curious reader, in search of what may charm him, cannot help saying: " This was all well enough, since the letters of the Portuguese Nun came of it."[1]

This war, which lasted until 1668, and in which Portugal triumphed, is indeed quite forgotten! The Portuguese Letters, on the contrary, have passed through twenty editions, and their great success is still undiminished. This is due above all

1 Saint Beuve, Notice of Mlle. Aïssé

to the accent of sincerity in the writer. The poor nun of Beja has painted with such fire, with so contagious an emotion, the state of her wounded heart, her helplessness, her fleeting hopes and persisting passion, her endless and cruel disappointments, and her legitimate anger, that we eagerly read and read again a correspondence whose ardent and touching pages remain ever fresh because they are absolutely true.

That which adds another charm to the letters of Marianna Alcaforado is the fact, so plain to be seen, that they were not written for publication. Oh no! these transports, this deep sadness, these avowals and bitter complaints have nothing studied about them. Here is the cry of a loyal and tender soul, and the reader is at once interested in such love mingled with such despair!

A few lines will suffice to sketch the drama which gave rise to the Portuguese Letters.

In 1661, Noël Bouton de Chamilly, Count of St. Leger (afterwards Marquis of Chamilly), took service in Portugal. He was then twenty-five years of age. At the same time a convent of the city of Beja sheltered the Franciscan nun, whose life, alas! was so profoundly disturbed by the young French captain.

Our heroine, who belonged to one of the best families of the country, relates how she saw M. de Chamilly for the first time from a balcony of her convent, and a learned critic, M. Eugène Asse, gives us reason to believe that she no doubt saw him upon the occasion of some review or triumphal entry of the Franco-Portuguese troops into Beja.

However this may be, M. de Chamilly having also, on his part, been attracted by the charming nun, visited the convent several times and gained the heart of the unfortunate Marianna, who until her last hour tried vainly to curse the brilliant officer whose desertion, so sudden and complete, broke her too confiding heart.

Let us add that the Marquis de Chamilly married, in 1677, the daughter of Jean-Jacques du Bouchet, Seigneur of Villefix, without the slightest concern for the nun of Beja, and that he was made a marshal of France in 1703, "in recompense of glorious service." After all, there is nothing very new or original in all this! An officer, elegant and noble, occupied his leisure hours in a little town in betraying an over-credulous young girl of rare beauty. Then, impatient to forget his vows, as soon as he left the country he wisely married an heiress. What can be more natural! Does this not happen every day?

And as the Maréchal de Chamilly, — a valiant soldier, except for this sin of his youth, — had no serious fault to reproach himself with, his contemporaries, St. Simon at their head, with one accord rendered him homage: "He was the best man in the world, the bravest, the most honorable."

These words are well chosen indeed! Happily, women have united to avenge the memory of Marianna, and no woman has ever forgiven the Marquis of Chamilly for his false promises and his irreparable levity, — in a word, his betrayal.

We must read these letters carefully on account of their very simplicity and naïve eloquence.

What exquisite tenderness, what profound grief! And suddenly, at the remembrance of happy hours forever gone, how the poor, forsaken girl revives in so touching a manner, forgetting, all at once, for too short a moment, the ingratitude and perfidy of her lover.

Love, regret: This is the whole book, — which will not die, because it is pervaded with the suave perfume of youth, of passion, and sincere tears.

–Alexandre Piedagnel, 1890

I

THINK, MY LOVE, to what an extent you have been wanting in foresight. Oh! unhappy man, you have been betrayed, and have betrayed me by false hopes. A passion upon which you had planned so much happiness now causes you a mortal despair, which can be compared only to the cruelty of the absence which occasions it. What! This absence, — for which my grief with all its ingenuity can find no name dark enough — will then forever prevent me from looking into those eyes where I saw so much love, and which made me conscious of feelings that filled me with joy, that took the place of everything, and left me satisfied.

Alas! my eyes are deprived of the only light which could brighten them; for them, tears alone remain, and the only use I have made of them is to weep unceasingly, since I learned that you had finally resolved upon a separation, so unbearable that it will soon kill me. Yet it seems to me that I cling to sorrows of which you alone are the cause. I gave my life to you as soon as I saw you, and I feel a certain pleasure in sacrificing it to you. A thousand times a day my sighs go out to you, seeking you everywhere, and bringing back in return for such disquietude only too true a warning, sent by my evil fortune, which is cruel enough not to let me deceive myself, but keeps saying, "Cease, cease, unhappy Marianna, vainly devouring your own heart, and searching for a lover whom you will never find; who has crossed the seas to escape from you; who is in France, in the midst of pleasures; who never gives a thought to your grief, and is quite willing to dispense with all these transports for which he is not in the least grateful." But no, I cannot make up my mind to judge you so harshly; I am too interested in justifying you; I will not let myself think that you have forgotten me. Am I not unhappy enough without tormenting myself with false suspicions? And why should I make the effort not to remember all the pains you took to prove to me your love. I was so charmed by all you did for me that I should be most ungrateful did I not love you with the same ardor that my passion aroused when you gave me proof of yours.

How is it possible that the memory of such delightful moments can become so cruel? Contrary to their nature, must they serve only to torture my very soul?

Alas! your last letter brought me to a strange condition; my heart suffered so keen a pang, that it seemed to make the effort to tear itself away from me and go in search of you. I was so overcome by these violent emotions that I remained more than three hours entirely without consciousness. I forbade myself to return to a life which I ought to lose for you, since I cannot keep it for you. I finally saw the light again in spite of myself. I flattered myself with the thought that I was dying of love, and moreover I was glad to be no longer exposed to have my heart torn by the grief of your absence. Since then I have suffered many other woes, but can I ever be without ills so long as I cannot see you? I bear them, however, without murmuring, since they come from you. What! is this then the reward you give me for having loved you so tenderly? But no matter, I am resolved to adore you all my life and never to look at any one else. And I assure you that you will do well also to love no one else. Could you be content with a passion less ardent than mine? You will find, perhaps, more beauty (although you used to call me beautiful), but you will never find so much love, and all the rest is nothing.

Do not fill your letters with useless things, do not write to me to remember you. I cannot forget you, and also I do not forget that you have allowed me to hope that you would come and spend some time with me. Alas! why will you not spend all your life here? If it were possible for me to leave this wretched cloister, I should not await in Portugal the fulfilment of your promises. I should go, regardless of consequences, to seek you, — to follow you and love you all the world over. I do not dare flatter myself that this is possible. I will not foster hopes which would certainly give me pleasure, and I will no longer be sensible to anything but pain.

I confess, however, that the opportunity given me by my brother to write to you, surprised in me a feeling of joy, and held in check, for a moment, my despair.

I conjure you to tell me why you set your heart upon fascinating me as you did, when you knew very well that you were going to desert me? and why have you been so pitiless in making me wretched? Why did you not leave me in peace in this cloister? Had I done you any injury! But forgive me; I impute nothing to you. I am in no state to think of revenge, and I only accuse the harshness of my fate. In separating us, it seems to have done all the harm we could have feared. But our hearts cannot be separated; love, which is more powerful than destiny, has united them for our whole life. If you take any interest in mine, write to me often. I certainly deserve to have you take some trouble in letting me know the state of your heart and your fortunes. Above all, come to see me. Farewell, I cannot leave this paper; it will fall into your hands; would that I might have the same happiness. Alas! how insane I am! I see that this is not possible. Farewell! I can write no more. Farewell, love me always and make me suffer still more misery.

II

IT SEEMS TO me that I do the greatest wrong in the world to the feelings of my heart, in trying to make them known to you in writing. How happy I should be if you could judge of them by the violence of your own! But I cannot expect anything from you, and I cannot help telling you, much less earnestly than I feel it, that you ought not to ill-treat me as you do, by a neglect which overwhelms me with despair, and which is even shameful in you. It is at least only just that you should let me complain of the woes which I so clearly foresaw, when I found you determined to leave me. I realize that I deceived myself when I thought that you would act in better faith than is usual, because the excess of my love seemed to lift me above any kind of suspicion and to deserve more fidelity than is ordinarily to be met with. But the desire you have to betray me overmasters the justice you owe to all I have done for you. I should not cease to be very unhappy if you loved me only because I love you, and I should wish to owe everything to your inclination alone; but this is so far from being the case that I have not received a single letter from you in six months. I attribute all this misfortune to the blindness of my attachment to you. Ought I not to have foreseen that my happiness would come to an end, rather than my love?

Could I hope that you would spend all your life in Portugal, and that you would renounce your fortune and your country to think only of me? My pain is without solace, and the remembrance of my pleasures fills me with despair.

What then! my desires are of no avail? And I shall never see you in my room again, giving way to all the ardor of your passion. But alas! I deceive myself, and I know only too well that the emotions which filled my mind and heart were with you but transitory, gone with the pleasure of the moment. In those too happy moments I should have called reason to my aid to moderate the fatal excess of my delight, and to predict all my present suffering. But I gave myself entirely to you, and was in no state to think of that which might poison all my happiness, and prevent me from enjoying to the full all the ardent proofs of your passion. I was too blissfully conscious that I was with you to think that some day you would be gone. Although I remember having told you sometimes that you would make me miserable; but these fears were soon dissipated, and I took pleasure in sacrificing them to you, and giving myself up to the enchantment and the bad faith of your protestations. I see very plainly the remedy for all my ills, and I should soon be delivered from them if I no longer loved you. But alas! what a remedy!

No, I would rather suffer still more than forget you. Alas! does this depend upon me? I. cannot reproach myself with having wished for a single moment not to go on loving you. You are more to be pitied than I. It is better to suffer all that I suffer, than to enjoy the languid pleasures that the women in France may give you. I do not envy you your indifference, and I pity you. I defy you to forget me utterly; I flatter myself that I have made it so that you can only experience imperfect enjoyment without me; and I am happier than you, because I am busier.

I have lately been made portress of the convent; every one who speaks to me thinks I am crazy. I do not know how I answer; and the nuns must be as crazy as I, to think me capable of taking care of anything.

Ah! I envy the happiness of Francisque and Emmanuel.[1] Why am I not always with you as they are ? I should have followed and served you more faithfully. I wish for nothing in this world but to see you. At least, remember me! I could content myself with your remembrance, but I dare not be sure of it. I did not limit my hopes to your remembrance when I saw you every day; but you have made me understand that I must submit to your will in everything. Still I do not regret having adored you; I am even glad to have been betrayed by you; your absence-harsh and perhaps eternal though it be-in no way diminishes the ardor of my love. I wish every one to know it. I make no mystery of it, and am only too happy to have done all that I have for you

---

1 Two little Portuguese servants belonging to M. Chamilly. [Translator's note]

in defiance of all propriety. I have made it my honor and my religion to love you desperately, since I have begun by loving you. I do not say all this to oblige you to write to me. Ah! do not force yourself in any way. I wish nothing from you which does not come of your free will, and I refuse all tokens of your love which you could help giving. I shall take pleasure in excusing you, because perhaps you will take pleasure in not taking pains to write to me; and I feel the deepest inclination to forgive all your faults. A French officer was charitable enough to talk to me more than three hours this morning about you; he told me that the peace of France was concluded. If this is true could you not come to see me, and take me back with you to France? But I do not deserve it. Do what you will; my love no longer depends on the way you may treat me. Since you went away I have not had a moment of health, and my only pleasure consists in naming your name a thousand times a day. Some of the nuns, who know to what a deplorable state you have reduced me, often talk to me about you.

I go as little as possible out of my room where you have come so many times to see me, and I look incessantly at your portrait, which is a thousand times dearer to me than my life. It gives me some pleasure but it also gives me great pain when I think that I may never see you again. How can it be possible that I shall never see you again? Have you abandoned me forever?

I am in despair. Your poor Marianna can bear no more. She faints in ending this letter. Farewell, farewell! Take pity on me.

III

WHAT WILL BECOME of me? and what would you have me do? I find myself very far removed from anything I had anticipated. I hoped that you would write to me from every place you passed through, and that your letters would be very long; that you would sustain my passion by the hope of seeing you again; that an entire confidence in your fidelity would give me some sort of repose and that in this way I should remain in a bearable enough condition, without extreme suffering. I had even thought of some feeble plans of making every effort I could to cure myself, if I became quite convinced that you had entirely forgotten me. Your absence, some devout aspirations, the fear of completely ruining the little health left to me after such watching and anxiety, the improbability of your return, the coldness of your last farewell, your departure, based on such cruel pretexts, and a thousand other reasons, only too good and too useless, seemed to promise me a sure aid, if necessary. In a word, having only myself to fight against, I never could have suspected all my weakness, nor apprehended all I suffer today. Alas, how much I am to be pitied that I cannot share my sorrows with you, and that I must be unhappy all alone. This thought kills me, and I die with the dread that perhaps you never really cared seriously for our happiness together. Yes, I realize now the bad faith of all your proceedings: you were deceiving me every time you told me that you were enraptured to be alone with me. Your ardor and transports were due only to my importunity; you had planned in cold blood to kindle my passion; you looked upon it only as a conquest and your heart was never deeply touched. Are you not indeed unfortunate, and do you not show very little delicacy in finding no other profit in my devotion? And how is it possible that with so much love I should not have been able to make you completely happy? I regret, for my very love of you, the infinite pleasures you have lost. Can it be that you did not desire them?

Ah, if you only knew them, you would have found in them, beyond a doubt, a far keener joy than in deceiving me; and you would have realized that one is much happier, and conscious of something much more touching, in loving violently than in being loved. I know not what I am, nor what I do, nor what I desire. I am torn by a thousand conflicting emotions. Can any one imagine a more deplorable condition ? I love you to distraction, and yet I would spare you so much that I would not even dare to wish you to be agitated by the same transport. I should kill myself, or die of grief without killing myself, if I were assured that you never have any peace, that your life is only trouble and agitation, that you weep unceasingly, and that everything is hateful to you. I cannot bear my own woes; how then could I stand the pain which yours would give me, and which would be a thousand times more intense? However, I cannot make up my mind, all the same, to wish you not to think of me; and, to speak sincerely, I am furiously jealous of everything which gives you pleasure, and which touches your heart or your fancy in France.

I do not know why I write to you. I see very plainly that you will only take pity on me, and I do not want your pity. I despise myself when I think of all that I have sacrificed for you. I have lost my reputation; I have exposed myself to the anger of my family, to the severity of the laws of the country against nuns, and to your ingratitude, which appears to me the greatest of all misfortunes. But I am well aware that my remorse is not real; that with all my heart I would gladly have risked still greater dangers for love of you, and that I take a fatal pleasure in having put my life and honor at stake. All that I have of most precious, might it not be at your disposal? And ought I not be very glad to have used it as I have? It even seems to me that I am not at all satisfied either with my grief or the excess of my love, although, alas! I certainly cannot flatter myself so far as to be satisfied with you. I live, faithless creature that I am, and do as much to preserve my life as to lose it. Ah, I could die of shame; my despair is only in my letters then.

If I loved you as much as I have told you a thousand times, should I not have died long ago? I have deceived you; it is for you to complain of me. Alas! why do you not complain? I saw you go away, I can never hope to see you return; and still I breathe! I have betrayed you. I ask your forgiveness, but do not grant it. Treat me harshly; reproach me that my emotions are not powerful enough; be more difficult to please; write to me that you wish me to die of love for you; and I entreat you to help me in this way, so that I may overcome the weakness of my sex and finish all this irresolution by a genuine despair. A tragic end would no doubt oblige you to think often about me; my memory would grow dear to you, and you would perhaps be deeply touched by an extraordinary death. Would not this be better than the state to which you have brought me? Farewell, would that I had never seen you! Ah, how well I know the falseness of this sentiment, and at the very moment of writing you, I recognize that I would infinitely rather be unhappy in loving you, than never to have seen you. I submit then without murmuring to my evil destiny, since you were not willing to make it a happier one. Farewell; promise to regret me tenderly, if I should die of grief; and at least let the violence of my passion make everything indifferent or distasteful to you. This consolation would be enough for me; and if I have to give you up forever, I would not leave you to another. Would it not be very cruel indeed of you to make use of my despair in order to render yourself more attractive, and show that you have inspired the greatest passion in the world? Farewell again. I write you too long letters; I have not sufficient consideration for you; I ask your forgiveness, and dare to hope that you will have some indulgence for a poor crazed girl, who, as you very well know, was sane enough before she loved you. Farewell, it seems to me that I talk to you too much of my unbearable condition; nevertheless, I thank you from the bottom of my heart for the despair you cause me, and I despise the tranquility in which I lived before knowing you. Farewell, my passion grows with every moment. Ah, how many things I have to say to you!

IV

YOUR LIEUTENANT HAS just told me that a storm obliged you to stop in the kingdom of Algarve. I fear that you may have suffered a great deal on the sea, and this dread has so haunted me that I could no longer think of all my own ills. Are you so convinced that your lieutenant takes more interest than I in all that happens to you? Why is he better informed, and pray why have you not written to me? I am truly unfortunate if you have found no opportunity since your departure; but still more so if you have found one, and not written! Your injustice and ingratitude are extreme, but I should be in despair if they brought any misfortune upon you, and I much prefer that they should go unpunished, rather than that I should be avenged. I resist all appearances which ought to convince me that you have no love for me, and I am much more disposed to yield blindly to my passion, than to the reasons you give me to complain of your want of affection. How much suffering you would have spared me if your conduct had been as indifferent the first days I saw you as it has seemed to me lately. But who would not have been deceived, like me, by such devotion, and who would not have thought it sincere? How hard it is to bring oneself to suspect the sincerity of those one loves! I see plainly that the least excuse is enough for you; and without your taking the trouble to make any, my love serves you so faithfully that I can only consent to find you guilty in order to enjoy the keen pleasure of justifying you myself. You overwhelmed me by your assiduity; you kindled me by your transports; you charmed me by your attentions; you reassured me by your vows; my own violent inclination carried me away, and the results of that beginning, so delightful and so happy, are only tears, sighs, and a tragic death, for all of which I can see no remedy. It is true that I have known the most surprising pleasure in loving you, but it costs me strange pangs as well, and all the emotions you inspire in me are extreme.

If I had obstinately resisted your love; if I had given you any cause of annoyance or jealousy, in order to arouse your passion; if you had perceived any artifice in my conduct; finally, if I had tried to oppose my reason to the natural inclination I had for you, which you very soon made me aware of (although my efforts would no doubt have been useless), you might have punished me severely and made use of your power; but you attracted me before you told me that you loved me; you gave me evidence of a great passion; I was carried away by it, and gave myself up to loving you desperately. You were not blinded like me, why then did you let me fall into the state I am in?

What did you want of all my ardent demonstrations, which could only be importunate to you ? You knew very well that you would not remain in Portugal; and why did you choose me here to make me so unhappy? You could certainly have found in this country some more beautiful woman, with whom you might have had as much pleasure, since you were only in search of that; who would have loved you faithfully as long as you were in sight; whom time would have consoled for your absence, and whom you might have left without perfidy and cruelty. Such conduct is much more that of a tyrant bent upon persecuting, than of a lover whose only thought is to please. Alas! why are you so pitiless with a heart that is all your own? I see very plainly that you are as easily influenced against me, as I was in your favor. I should have resisted, without needing all my love, and without thinking I had done anything extraordinary, stronger reasons than any that could have compelled you to leave me. They would have seemed to me very weak, and not one of them could have ever torn me away from you; but you were glad to take advantage of any pretext you could find to return to France. A vessel was sailing. Why did you not let it sail? Your family had written to you. Do you not know all the persecutions I have borne from mine? Your honor forced you to leave me. Had I taken any care of mine? You were obliged to go serve your king. If all that is said of him be true, he had no need of your help and he would have excused you. I should have been too happy if we could have passed our lives together; but since a cruel absence had to separate us, it seems to me that

29

I ought to be very glad not to have been faithless, nor would I for anything in the world have committed so base an action.

What! You knew the depths of my heart and my tenderness, and you could resolve to leave me forever, and expose me to the dread, I must necessarily feel, that you should only remember me to sacrifice me to a new passion. I realize that I love you madly; however, I do not complain of the extravagant desires of my heart; I am accustomed to its persecutions; and I could not live were it not that I discover and enjoy a secret pleasure in loving you in the midst of a thousand pains. But I am constantly persecuted in the most distressing way by the hatred and disgust I feel for everything. My family, my friends, and this convent are insupportable to me. Everything that I am obliged to see, and everything that I must of necessity do, is odious to me. I am so jealous of my love that it seems to me as though all my actions and duties only concerned you. Yes, I feel a certain scruple in not devoting every moment of my life to you. What should I do, alas! without all this hatred and all this love which fill my heart? Could I survive what occupies me so incessantly and lead a dull and tranquil life? I could not endure the emptiness and indifference.

Every one has noticed the complete change in my disposition, my manners, and my person. My mother spoke to me about it with harshness, and then with some kindness. I do not know how I answered her. I think I confessed everything to her. The most severe nuns pity the state I am in; it even inspires them with some respect and attention for me. Every one is touched by my love, and you remain profoundly indifferent, only writing me cold letters, full of repetitions; half the paper is not filled, and you make it grossly apparent that you are dying to come to the end.

Doña Brites tormented me a few days ago, to leave my room, and thinking to divert me took me for a walk on the balcony, from which Mertola can be seen; I followed and was immediately struck by a cruel remembrance, which made me weep all the rest of the day. She brought me back, and I threw myself on my bed, where I made a thousand reflections as to the improbability of my ever being cured. What is done to comfort me sharpens my grief, and in the very remedies, I find special reasons to be more afflicted. I have often seen you pass by that place with an air which charmed me, and I stood on that balcony the fatal day when I felt the first intimations of my unhappy passion. It seemed to me that you wished to please me, although you did not know me; I was convinced that you had remarked me among all who were with me. I imagined, when you stopped, that you were very glad I could see you better and could admire the skill with which you managed your horse. I was surprised into some alarm when you rode him into a dangerous place; in fact I was secretly interested in all your actions. I felt sure that you were not indifferent to me, and I took everything you did, to myself. You know only too well the consequences of all these beginnings; and although I have nothing to conceal, I must not write them to you, for fear of making you more guilty if possible than you are, and of having to reproach myself with so many useless efforts to force you to be faithful to me. You will never be so. Can I hope from my letters and reproaches an influence which my love and my complete surrender could not call forth from your ingratitude? I am too assured of my misfortune; your unfair behavior does not leave me the least reason to doubt it, and I have everything to apprehend since you have deserted me. Will you have charms only for me, and will you not appear agreeable in other eyes than mine? I think I should not be sorry if the sentiments of others justified my own in some way, and I should like all the women in France to find you attractive, but none to love you, and none to please you.

This idea is ridiculous and impossible; moreover I have been made fully aware that you are not capable of any persistency, and that you will easily forget me, without any assistance and without being impelled to it by a new passion. Perhaps I should like you to have some reasonable pretext. I should be more unhappy, it is true, but you would not be so guilty. I can plainly see that you will live in France without intense pleasures, but with entire freedom; the fatigue of a long journey, some petty conventionality, and the fear of not responding to my passion, keep you back. Ah, do not be alarmed about me. I shall be contented to see you from time to time and just to know that we are in the same place; but perhaps I flatter myself and you may be more touched by the harshness and severity of another woman than you have been by my affection. Is it possible that your ardor is kindled by unkind treatment? But before involving yourself in a serious passion stop to think of the excess of my grief, the uncertainty of my plans, the conflict of my emotions, the extravagance of my letters, my trust, my despair, my longings, and my jealousy. Ah, you are going to make yourself very unhappy; I entreat you to profit by the state I am in, and at least to let what I suffer for you not be useless to you.

Five or six months ago you made me an unfortunate confidence, and confessed to me too frankly that you had loved a lady in your country. If she prevents you from coming back, let me know it without delay, so that I may pine no longer. A little remnant of hope still sustains me, and if it is not to be fulfilled, I should be very glad to lose it completely and lose myself with it. Send me her portrait and one of her letters, and write me all she says to you. Perhaps I might find reasons for being consoled or still more profoundly afflicted. I can no longer remain in my present condition, and there is no change which would not be for the better. I should also like to have the portrait of your brother and sister-in-law. All that is of any interest to you is very dear to me, and I am entirely devoted to whatever comes near to you; I have given up all disposition of myself. There are moments when it seems as though I could be submissive enough to serve the woman you love. Your unkindness and neglect have so crushed me that sometimes I hardly dare think I can ever be jealous of you for fear of displeasing you, and I seem to be doing the greatest wrong in the world in reproaching you. I am often convinced that I ought not recall to you with such frenzy as I do the sentiments which you disown.

An officer has been waiting a long time for this letter. I had resolved to write it in such a way as not to make you dislike to receive it, but it is too extravagant, and I must finish it. Alas! I cannot bring myself to do this; it seems as if I were talking to you when I write, and, as if you were a little nearer. My first letter you will not find so long or so importunate; you may open and read it with this assurance. It is true that I ought not speak to you of a passion which displeases you, and I will no longer speak of it. In a few days, it will be a year since I gave myself up to you entirely and without reserve. Your passion seemed to me very ardent and sincere, and I should never have thought that my favors could have repelled you so as to oblige you to travel five hundred leagues and expose yourself to shipwreck in order to avoid them; certainly I did not deserve such treatment from any one. You may remember my modesty, my shame, and confusion; but you do not remember what ought to bind you to love me in spite of yourself.

The officer who is to carry this letter to you sends me word for the fourth time that he must leave. What haste he is in! Doubtless he is forsaking some unhappy girl in this country. Farewell, — it is harder for me to finish my letter than it was for you to leave me, perhaps for ever. Farewell, — I dare not give you a thousand tender names, nor give way without restraint to all my feelings. I love you a thousand times more than my life and a thousand times more than I know. How dear you are to me and how cruel! you never write to me; I could not help saying that again. I am beginning all over again, and the officer will start. What does it matter, let him start? I am writing more for myself than for you; I am only trying to console myself. Moreover the length of my letter will frighten you; so you will not read it. What have I done to be so unhappy, and why have you poisoned my life? Why was I not born in another country? Farewell, forgive me; I no longer dare beg you to love me; see to what my fate has brought me! Farewell.

V

I WRITE TO you for the last time and I hope to make you understand by the difference in tone and manner of this letter that you have at last convinced me that you no longer love me, and that therefore I must no longer love you. I shall send you back then, by the first opportunity, all that I have of yours. Do not fear that I will write to you; I shall not even put your name on the package. I have intrusted all this detail to Doña Brites, whom I had accustomed to confidences of a very different nature; I can trust her better than myself. She will take all necessary precautions to enable me to be sure that you have received the portrait and the bracelets you gave me. I want you to know, however, that for the last few days I have felt like destroying those little tokens of your love which were so dear to me; but I have shown you so much weakness that you would never believe me capable of such an extremity. So then I shall enjoy all the pain of parting from them and cause you at least some chagrin. I confess, to my shame and yours, that I found myself caring more for these trifles than I dare tell you, and that I had fresh need of all my resolution to give up each one individually, even when I flattered myself that I no longer cared for you — but one can succeed in anything one attempts with so many good reasons. I put them in the hands of Doña Brites.

How many tears this decision has cost me! After a thousand emotions and a thousand uncertainties of which you can have no knowledge, and of which assuredly I shall give you no account, I entreated her never to speak of them to me, never to give them back to me even if I should ask to see them once more, and to return them to you without letting me know. I have only realized the excess of my love since I have been using all my efforts to cure myself; and I fear that I should never have dared to undertake it, if I could have foreseen so many difficulties and such violence. I am convinced that I should have had less distress in loving you, ungrateful as you are, than in leaving you forever. I have discovered that you were less dear to me than my passion, and I have suffered strangely in combating it, even after your outrageous conduct had made you personally hateful to me.

The ordinary pride of my sex has not helped me to take a stand against you. Alas! I have endured your contempt; I could have borne your hatred and all the jealousy that your attachment to another might have caused me. I should at least have had a passion of some sort to fight against; but your indifference is insupportable. Your impertinent protestations of friendship and the ridiculous civilities of your last letter showed me that you had received all those I had written: that they aroused no emotion in your heart, and that yet you read them. Ungrateful man! I am still insane enough to be in despair at not being able to flatter myself that they never reached you and were not delivered to you. I detest your frankness. Did I beg you to write me sincerely the truth? Why did you not leave me my passion? All you had to do was, not to write to me: I did not wish to be enlightened. Am I not most unfortunate in having been unable to force you to take some pains to deceive me, and in no longer having it in my power to excuse you? Know that I recognize that you are unworthy of any of my sentiments, and that I see all your evil qualities. However (if all I have done for you can deserve some little regard for the favor I ask), I conjure you not to write me again, and to help me to forget you utterly. If you were to express to me, however feebly, that you felt any pain in reading this letter, I might believe you perhaps; and then again perhaps your acknowledgment and acquiescence might arouse my anger and resentment, and all this might rekindle my passion. Do not interfere then with my action; you would doubtless overthrow all my plans in whatever way you tried to enter into them. I do not wish to know the effect of this letter; do not disturb the state of mind I am preparing for myself; it seems as though you ought to be content with the wretchedness you cause me (whatever may have been your design to make me unhappy). Do not deprive me of my uncertainty; in time I hope it may grow tranquil. I promise not to hate you! I have too great a distrust of any violent feeling to dare indulge in it.

I am quite sure that I might find perhaps, in this country, a more faithful lover; but alas, who could inspire me with love? Would the passion of another affect me? Has mine had any power over you? Do I not realize that a heart which has been deeply moved, never forgets what has awakened it to transports of which it was unconscious, and yet capable; that all its desires are bound up in the idol it has made; that its first impressions, and its first wounds can neither be cured nor effaced; that all the passions which would come to its aid, and attempt to fill and satisfy it, vainly promise a sensibility which it can never feel again; that all the pleasures it seeks, without any wish to find them, only serve to prove that nothing is so dear to it as the remembrance of its grief. Why have you made known to me the imperfection and dissatisfaction of an attachment which cannot be eternal, and the misfortunes which follow a violent passion when it is not reciprocated? And why do a cruel fate and a blind inclination always persist in making us set our hearts upon those who would be attracted by some one else?

Even though I might hope for some amusement in a new engagement, and might find a person of good faith, I have so much pity for myself that I would have many scruples before bringing the poorest wretch in the world to the state you have left me in; and although I have no reason to spare you, I could never make up my mind to take so cruel a revenge upon you, even though it were to depend upon me, through a change of feeling which I do not anticipate.

I am trying now to excuse you, and I can very well understand that nuns are not usually lovable. However, it seems to me that if one were capable of reasoning about one's choice, it would be better to become attached to them than to other women. Nothing prevents them from thinking unceasingly about their passion; they are not diverted by a thousand things which absorb and distract in the world. It seems to me that it is not very pleasant to see the woman one loves, always occupied with a thousand trifles; and one must have very little delicacy (or else be in despair) in allowing them to talk only about dress, assemblies, and entertainments. There is constant cause for jealousy; they are obliged to show attentions, to make themselves charming and agreeable in conversation. Who can be sure that they do not take pleasure in these occasions? Ah, how they should mistrust a lover who does not exact the strictest account of all this, who believes readily and without misgiving all they tell him, and who sees them, with entire confidence and tranquillity, subject to all these calls. But I do not expect to prove to you by good reasons that you ought to love me; this would be a poor way indeed, and I have tried a much better one without success. I know too well my destiny to attempt to overcome it; I shall be unhappy all my life. Was I not so, even when I saw you every day! I was in deadly fear that you might not be faithful to me; I wished to see you every moment, and this was not possible; I was anxious on account of the danger you ran in coming into the convent; I could scarcely live when you were with the army; I was in despair at not being more beautiful and more worthy of you; I murmured against the insignificance of my position; I often thought that the attachment you appeared to have for me might be an injury to you; it seemed to me that I did not love you enough; I dreaded the anger of my parents for you, and in fact I was in as pitiable a condition as I am at present. If you had given me any proof of your passion since you went away from Portugal, I should have made every effort to leave here; I should have disguised myself and gone to meet you.

Alas! what would have become of me if you had not cared for me after I had got to France? What misery! What madness! What a depth of shame for my family who have grown so dear to me since I no longer love you! You can see now that I have the sense to realize that it would be possible for me to be more wretched than I am; and I am speaking to you reasonably for once in my life. How pleased you will be at my moderation; and how well satisfied with me! But I wish to know nothing about it; I have already begged you never to write to me again, and I entreat it once more.

Have you never reflected upon the way you have treated me? Does it never occur to you that you are under greater obligations to me than to any one in the world? I have loved you to madness. What contempt I had for everything else! Your conduct is not that of an honorable man. You must have had a natural aversion for me, or you would have loved me desperately; I have been fascinated by very ordinary qualities. What have you done to please me? What sacrifice have made for me?

Did you not seek a thousand other pleasures? Have you given up gaming and hunting? Were you not the first to rejoin the army, and the last to return from it? You exposed yourself, recklessly, although I begged you for my sake to be careful. You took no measures to establish yourself in Portugal, where you were respected. A letter from your brother called you away without a moment's hesitation; and do I not know that during the voyage you were in the best possible spirits ?

I must acknowledge that I ought to hate you mortally. Ah, I have brought all my misfortunes upon myself. From the first I accustomed you to my desperate passion with utter sincerity, and one must learn to be artful in order to be loved, one must be clever enough to find a way to excite feeling in others, and love alone does not beget love . You determined that I should love you ; and as you had formed this design, you would have left nothing undone to accomplish it. You would have even made up your mind to love me, if that had been necessary; but you found out that you could succeed in your undertaking without passion , and that you had no need of it.

What perfidy! Do you think you have deceived me with impunity? If any chance brought you back to this country, I declare to you that I would give you up to the vengeance of my family. I lived for a long time in an abandonment and idolatry which fill me with horror now, and my remorse pursues me without pity. I feel keenly the shame of the crimes you made me commit, and alas! I have no longer the passion which prevented me from seeing their enormity. When will my heart cease to be torn? When shall I be delivered from this cruel position? However, I believe that I do not wish you any ill, and that I could even consent to your happiness; but how can you be happy if your heart is what it should be?

I want to write you another letter, to show you that after a while I shall be more tranquil perhaps. How much pleasure I shall take in being able to reproach you for your unjust dealing, when I no longer feel it so keenly; and when I can make you understand that I despise you, that I speak with indifference of your treachery, that I have forgotten all my sorrows and all my joys, and that I only remember you when I wish to remember you. I acknowledge that you have a great advantage over me, and that you inspired me with a passion which deprived me of my reason; but you need not be too much flattered. I was young, I was credulous, and had been shut up in this convent since my childhood; I had only seen disagreeable people; I had never heard the praises which you lavished upon me incessantly; it seemed as if I owed to you the charms and the beauty which you found in me, and of which you made me conscious; I heard you well spoken of; every one had some. thing to say in your favor; you did all that was needed to inspire me with love. But at last I have awakened from my enchantment; you have given me great help, and I confess that I needed it to the utmost. In sending you back your letters, I shall carefully keep the last two you wrote me; and I shall read them over and over again oftener than I read the first, so that I may not fall back into my weakness. Ah! how much they cost me, and how happy I should have been if you had only let me love you always! I know very well that I am still somewhat too concerned with my reproaches and your infidelity; but remember that I have promised myself a more peaceful state, and that I will attain it, or else that I shall take some extreme measure against myself, which you will hear without great distress. But I ask nothing more from you; how foolish I am to repeat the same things so often! I must leave you and think no more about you; perhaps even I shall not write to you again. Am I obliged to give you an exact account of all my varied emotions?

THE END

ABOUT THE AUTHOR

THE PORTUGUESE LETTERS were first published anonymously in 1669. A later edition that came out with the transcription: translated into French by Guilleragues. Gabriel-Joseph de Lavergne, viscount of Guilleragues, was then working in the service of the Louis XIV as a diplomat. Recent scholarship has identified Guilleragues as the author of these letters. It is generally believed today that the letters are a fictionalised account by Guilleragues himself, inspired by *Letters of Abelard and Héloïse*, and are not the actual love letters of the Portuguese nun from Beja, Mariana Alcoforado. He kept his identity secret as author of the letters as protection, although many of his famous literary friends, such as Racine and Boileau, knew.

BIBLIOGRAPHICAL NOTE

THE FIRST EDITION of the Portuguese Letters appeared in 1669, published by Claude Barbin. It contained these five original letters overflowing with passion and the grief caused by desertion. M. Eugène Asse thinks there is proof that the translation was furnished the publishers about the middle of the year 1668, almost immediately after the return of the Count de Chamilly to France.

"Evidently," says M. Asse, "the letters of poor Marianna were displayed by their possessor as trophies, or at least as among the souvenirs which one brings back from a foreign country."

Nevertheless the incognito was complete. It is only in the edition of 1690 that the name of the translator Guilleragues appears, and also that of the person to whom they were supposed to be addressed. The name of the heroine, discovered by the learned Boissonade in 1810, has never figured in any edition.

[A.P]